78892

3,4

1 point

SISKIYC

D0403062

# Sky Babies

## JUDY DELTON

*Illustrated by Alan Tiegreen*

A YEARLING BOOK

Published by
Bantam Doubleday Dell Books for Young Readers
a division of
Bantam Doubleday Dell Publishing Group, Inc.
1540 Broadway
New York, New York 10036

ISBN: 0-440-40530-0

Printed in the United States of America

November 1991

10  9  8  7  6

CWO

*For the baby in my life,*
*Daniel Jaschke Levy*

# Contents

# Contents

# CHAPTER 1

# Sonny's News

"Pee Wee, Pee Wee Scouts!" sang the Pee Wee Scouts. It was the last line of their Scout song. The Tuesday meeting for Troop 23 was over.

"Next week I'll have some news for you!" called their leader, Mrs. Peters. "News about a new badge we'll all earn. And news about Christmas and Hanukkah."

"I wonder what badge we get next,"

said Molly Duff to her best friend, Mary Beth Kelly, on the way home.

"Maybe it's a Christmas badge," said Mary Beth. "Or a winter badge. We could shovel sidewalks or something."

Shoveling sidewalks didn't sound like a fun thing to do to earn a badge. Molly hoped it would be a more fun badge than that.

"Maybe it will be a Christmas-shopping badge," said Molly. "Or a decorating-the-tree badge!"

Snow was beginning to fall. The sidewalks were getting slippery. It was easy to think about the holidays when it was snowing.

Roger White came sliding up behind the girls. He slid right into them and fell to the ground.

"Hey, I know what badge we're going to get," he said.

Roger must have been listening, thought Molly. How would he know, anyway? Mrs. Peters hadn't told anyone yet.

"The wrestling badge," he said. "We all have to wrestle each other."

Roger lay on the ground pretending to be a wrestler.

"I'm not going to wrestle!" said Mary Beth. "No one can make me."

"There's no such thing as a wrestling badge," said Molly, giving Roger a kick with the toe of her snowboot. "Quit making things up, Roger."

Molly didn't think there was a wrestling badge. But maybe Roger wasn't kidding. Maybe Mrs. Peters did have wrestling badges.

"After that we get a judo badge," Roger went on. "We get black belts so we can defend ourselves."

"I'm quitting Pee Wee Scouts," said Mary Beth. "I don't like that rough stuff."

"Don't believe him," said Molly. "He's making it all up."

Roger yelled, "Hi yah! Crash!" and pretended to break a tree branch across his knee.

"Hey, you guys, wait for me!" called Sonny Stone.

Sonny's last name used to be Betz. His mother used to be Mrs. Betz, the assistant Scout leader. But last year she married the fire chief, Larry Stone, and Sonny had a new father. So Sonny had a new name to match the fire chief's.

"You know what?" asked Sonny, all out of breath from running. "My mom's going to get a baby!"

"She already has a baby," said Roger. "You're her baby."

"She really is," said Sonny.

"I don't believe you," said Mary Beth. "Why didn't you tell us at Pee Wee Scouts?"

"Because it's a secret," said Sonny.

Molly didn't think Sonny would lie. Sonny was a baby, Roger was right. He still had training wheels on his bike. But he wasn't a liar.

"Hey, is the stork bringing it?" Roger laughed.

"Of course not," said Sonny. "I know the stork doesn't bring babies."

"I'll bet he thinks the doctor brings them in a black bag," whispered Mary Beth to Molly, giggling.

"I know where babies come from," said Sonny. "They come out of the sky. A plane brings them."

"Ho, ho, ho!" Roger chortled. "A plane's as dumb as a stork!"

"Babies grow in their mother's stomach," whispered Molly to Sonny. She hated it when people laughed at Sonny. Why didn't his parents tell him these things?

But Sonny shook his head. "They do not. They come from the sky. My mom told me."

Molly groaned. Could it be possible that Mrs. Stone didn't know herself where babies came from? She must. She had Sonny. And Sonny couldn't have come out of the sky on a plane.

"A big jet," Sonny was saying.

"Sure, sure," said Roger. "And he'll wear a seat belt and watch the movie on the way."

Roger turned the corner to his house, laughing.

Sonny turned at the next street. "Just wait and see," he called to them.

"He's never going to grow up," said Mary Beth. "I thought he'd be different once he had a dad. But he's still a mama's boy."

"See you in the morning," said Molly when they came to her house.

Mary Beth waved.

The next morning Molly got to school early. She waited for Mrs. Stone to drop Sonny off at the door as she always did.

"She doesn't look like she's going to have a baby," said Molly to Mary Beth later. "She isn't fat at all."

"Maybe she isn't having it for a long time," said Mary Beth.

At recess Sonny said, "My mom is getting the baby before Christmas."

"He is lying," said Mary Beth. "His mom isn't fat enough to have a baby by Christmas. My mom was out to here when she had babies."

Mary Beth showed Molly with her arms how far out her mom's stomach had come.

The next Tuesday at the Pee Wee Scout meeting, Sonny's mother was there to help. Her stomach was still flat as a pancake.

"I have loads of good news today," said Mrs. Peters to her troop. "My first good news is that Sonny's mother is expecting a baby by Christmas. In fact, she is expecting two babies, twins! Sonny is going to have a little brother and sister!"

The Scouts looked stunned.

"By Christmas?" asked Rachel Meyers. "Is she sure?"

"Twins?" said Patty and Kenny Baker together. They were the only twins whom Molly knew.

Mrs. Peters looked at the puzzled

Scouts. Mrs. Stone was pink and beaming.

"We're adopting them," she said. "They are from another country. They are coming before Christmas, and before Hanukkah. They are coming on a plane."

"See," said Sonny, pointing to Roger and Molly and Mary Beth. "I wasn't making it up. I know where babies come from. They come from the sky, on a plane. That stomach stuff is a lie."

# CHAPTER 2

# Twin Talk

**M**rs. Peters brought out the treats of cupcakes and soda pop right away. Even before the Scouts told about their good deeds.

"To celebrate!" she said. "Two new little Pee Wee Scouts!"

"It'll be a long time before they're old enough to be Pee Wee Scouts," said Kevin Moe. "Six whole years."

"Time goes fast," Mrs. Peters said,

laughing. "Babies grow up fast. Just look at Nick."

Nick was Mrs. Peters's baby. "Goo!" he said, shaking his rattle.

Molly didn't think time went fast. It seemed to drag. Especially when everyone else got his or her cupcake first. And it took forever to be Christmas, and summer vacation and her birthday.

"Well, old baby-face Stone put one over on us, didn't he?" said Roger to Molly.

"All babies don't come on planes," said Mary Beth. "These babies will, but Sonny thinks that's where all babies come from."

"Even these babies didn't come out of the sky," said Tracy Barnes. "They had to come out of some mother, even if they are adopted."

"Try and tell Sonny that," said Rachel, laughing.

**13**

Molly decided she wouldn't try to tell Sonny anything. Ever again. Every time she did, Sonny had the last word. He was a baby, but he was smart.

Mrs. Stone told the Scouts the twins were three months old. She held up a picture of them. They had rosy faces and dark hair.

"Which one is a boy?" asked Tim Noon.

"This one is Lee," said Mrs. Stone, pointing. "And this one is Lani."

"They look just alike," said Lisa Ronning.

"Twins all look alike," said Kenny.

"Most twins do," said Sonny's mother.

"We can't wait to see them, can we?" said Mrs. Peters.

Everyone cheered. Molly was happy for Sonny and his family. But she was sad for herself. Every one of the Pee Wees seemed to have brothers and sisters except her. Molly was an only child. Rachel was, too, but even she had a baby cousin who lived nearby. All the other Pee Wees had more children in the family. Molly always felt left out when she saw them baking cookies together and playing Monopoly. She didn't even have a brother to fight with.

And now Sonny went from having just his mother and himself, to a family of five! Why didn't her family adopt? Better yet, her mother could go to the hospital like other mothers and get a baby.

Mrs. Peters tapped a spoon on the table for attention.

"Now for the rest of our news," she said. "We are going to talk about our new badge today."

The Pee Wees cheered.

"I hope it's not wrestling," said Mary Beth.

**15**

"Or judo," said Molly.

"Our new badge," said Mrs. Peters, "comes just at the right time! It ties in with the new twins, and with the holidays!"

The Pee Wees cheered again.

What badge could tie in with new babies and Christmas both?

"Is it a badge for getting a baby a Christmas present?" asked Tracy. "Because I'm getting our baby a teddy bear."

"No, this is something you learn, not something you buy," said Mrs. Peters mysteriously. "It is a badge for baby-tending. We are going to learn how to help take care of a baby. In an emergency, all of you will know what to do."

"A fire is an emergency, Mrs. Peters," said Rachel. "I already know how to save my little cousin Rhonda if the house

**16**

burned down. I'd pick her up and run out the door to the neighbors'."

"Wrong," said Kevin. "You should call 911 to report the fire."

"Then the baby would burn up, dummy," said Lisa.

Mrs. Peters clapped her hands. "It's a good idea to get the baby out," she said. "Rachel is right."

Rachel stuck her tongue out at Kevin.

"But Kevin is right too. Then you could call 911 from the neighbors'," Mrs. Peters went on.

"Ha," said Kevin.

"To get our badge, we are going to learn other things too. We'll learn how to feed a baby and hold a baby and change a diaper," their leader said.

Roger held his nose and made a face. "I'm not changing any old diaper," he said.

Some of the other Pee Wees held their noses, too, and Mrs. Peters had to clap her hands again for silence.

"Most of you have small brothers and sisters or relatives. After we learn how to do these things, you can ask your mothers to let you help with their bath, and feeding and dressing. Then by the holidays we all may be able to give the gift of baby-sitting. You can help watch the baby while your mother cooks dinner or washes clothes. It's a gift you don't have to buy. It's something you can do."

"My mom will like that," said Mary Beth. "She always has a lot of work to do and she has to stop and rock the baby."

"My dad takes care of the baby," said Tracy. "He cooks and washes the clothes too."

"I already take care of my cousin

Rhonda," said Rachel. "I gave her a bottle twice."

Rat's knees, thought Molly. It *was* important that her mother get a baby and get one quick. But how could her mother have a baby by Christmas? She couldn't even adopt a baby that fast. Who would Molly practice with? Who would she give a baby-sitting present to? Would she be the only one without this badge?

Mrs. Stone passed out papers. On the paper was a list of things each Scout had to do to get the badge.

"We will do some of these things today with Nick, and then you can try it with your mother's help," said Mrs. Peters.

Mrs. Peters picked Nick up. She took a bottle of milk out of the refrigerator and heated it. She showed the Scouts how to hold a baby to give it a bottle, and how to test that it wasn't too hot. Some of the Scouts got to hold Nick and feed him. When Molly held him, he spit up. All over her Scout kerchief. Mrs. Peters sponged her off.

Roger held his nose.

Mrs. Stone showed the Scouts how to change a diaper.

"My aunt uses baby powder," said Rachel. "It smells real good."

"Powder or baby oil is fine," said Mrs. Peters, "if the mother says so."

"Goo," said Nick. He liked all this attention.

"Remember to keep babies away from hot stoves, and steps where they could fall," said Mrs. Stone. "When a baby walks or crawls, you have to watch him every moment. You can't take your eyes off a baby if you are in charge of him."

"I know all that stuff," whispered Rachel to Molly. "It's boring."

Molly frowned at Rachel to be quiet. She would give anything to have a sister or cousin to powder and bathe. She looked at the list Mrs. Stone had passed out. How would she be able to do these things without a baby? And how would she ever get a badge if she didn't do them?

# CHAPTER 3

# Out of the Sky

"**M**y," said Mrs. Peters. "The time went so fast today that we don't have time to tell our good deeds. They'll have to keep until next time."

"Good," said Roger to Molly. "I won't have to do any new ones this week."

"You should have twice as many good deeds to report next week," said their leader. Molly poked Roger.

The Scouts got into a big circle. They

said their Scout pledge. Then they sang their Scout song. Molly loved singing. She loved being a Scout. But where could she find a baby? If she didn't she might not be able to get this badge. And if she didn't get badges, she wouldn't be a Pee Wee Scout. She wouldn't be able to say the pledge with her friends. She wouldn't be able to sing the Scout song. Why were her parents so selfish? Her mother could have had a baby by now, from the hospital, or from a plane. And now it was too late.

On the way home, Molly told Mary Beth her problem.

"I'll share my baby," said Mary Beth generously. "We can both feed Jennifer."

"I want a baby of my own," said Molly. "But thank you."

The next morning at school, Sonny got out of Larry's fire truck yelling, "They're coming! They're coming!"

"Who's coming, dummy, the Russians?" asked Roger.

"The twins!" said Sonny. "They are coming this afternoon! I get off school to meet the plane."

Everyone gathered around Sonny. No one else had babies who came from the sky. Or who came on a plane. No one had a baby who was adopted.

Lucky Sonny, thought Molly. He'd get his badge right away. Maybe even tonight.

The next day Mrs. Peters phoned all of the Pee Wee Scouts. She talked to the mothers too.

"I thought we should call a special meeting on Saturday," she said. "It will be a Pee Wee baby shower at my house. All of you can make a pretty card to welcome the babies. We can meet the twins and have a little party to celebrate their arrival."

"I'm bringing two silver cups with their names on them," said Rachel to Molly on the phone. "My mom's getting them engraved at the jewelry store."

Rachel was a show-off, thought Molly.

"Mrs. Peters said we should bring a card," said Molly.

Rachel scoffed. "What's a baby shower without presents?" she said. "When my little cousin Rhonda was born I gave her a solid-gold locket."

On Saturday the parents brought presents. Mrs. Duff brought four little bibs. Mr. Kelly brought two circus toys with giraffes in the middle. Mrs. Ronning brought two sunsuits. "For next summer," she said.

Molly made a bright red card with a picture of two babies on it. The babies in the picture were in two cradles. One cradle said "Lee" on it and one said "Lani."

Sonny drew himself with his two new babies. Tim drew a picture of his own house with a brown crayon. Kevin was the only one with a store-bought card.

"Oh, look at them smile!" said Lisa.

"Lani has a tooth!" said Rachel. "Just like Rhonda."

"What a cute little itsy-bitsy baby," cooed Tracy.

Molly couldn't think of anything to say. She didn't know how to talk to babies.

Mrs. Stone passed the babies from mother to mother. Then Patty and Kenny and Tim took turns holding one. She even let Rachel give Lani a bottle.

Rachel tested the milk on her wrist. "I do this all the time," she said. "It can't be too warm or too cold."

When Lani had finished the milk, Rachel put a cotton towel over her shoulder.

"That's in case she spits up," said Kenny. "That's what we do when we hold our baby."

Rachel held the baby up and patted her back. The baby burped.

"Good for *you!*" cooed Rachel. "Babies have to burp," she explained. "Otherwise they have gas and get a stomachache."

There was no doubt about it, Rachel knew a lot about babies.

Everyone here knew a lot about babies. Even Molly's own mom.

"Would you like to hold the baby, Molly?" asked Mrs. Stone.

Molly shook her head. She didn't know how to hold a baby. What if Lani's head fell off? It looked very wobbly. What if she dropped the baby and it broke its arm?

"No, thank you," said Molly.

Mrs. Peters brought out little sandwiches in the shape of rattles. They ate them on plates that had pictures of storks on them. Then they had cake that said *Welcome twins* on the frosting. In the middle of Mrs. Peters's dining room table was a big diaper filled with flowers.

Molly was glad when it was time to go home. Molly didn't ride home with her mother. She walked home with Mary Beth.

On the way she kicked a soda can. Mary Beth knew what she was upset about.

"Maybe we should try to find you a baby," she said.

"Where?" said Molly.

Mary Beth shrugged her shoulders. "I don't know, but we have to look. Remember when we looked for fire hazards?"

Molly sighed. "Babies aren't just lying around like matches," she said. But Mary Beth was right. It didn't hurt to look.

"What we need to find is an orphan," said Mary Beth. "An orphan could be your very own to feed and dress."

That made sense to Molly. Parents wouldn't give up a baby. But if a baby had no parents . . .

The girls looked up and down the streets. They looked in parks.

"There's a baby!" shouted Molly.

The girls ran up to a toddler in a stroller. An older boy was pushing her.

"Is this your baby?" asked Molly.

"Does anyone own her?" asked Mary Beth.

The boy held tightly to the stroller.

"We own her," the boy said. "She's my little sister."

"She's too old anyway," said Mary Beth, trying to make Molly feel better. "She's probably walking. And she drinks out of a glass. You want a baby who takes a bottle."

The girls walked around three more blocks. They walked by the library. The only babies they saw were with mothers and fathers.

"Let's stop at the drugstore for a candy bar," said Mary Beth.

The drugstore was around the corner. It had a Christmas tree in the window. The tree was decorated with little bars of soap and boxes of Band-Aids.

"I'd sure hate to get Band-Aids for Christmas," said Molly.

"Look!" said Mary Beth. She pointed to a baby carriage in front of the drugstore. There was a baby in it, sleeping.

"That might be your baby," said Mary Beth.

The girls walked up to the carriage. The

baby had a little white snowsuit on. And a cap with a red tassel.

"It's nobody's," said Mary Beth. "It needs a home, I'll bet."

Molly looked doubtful. "Orphans don't have carriages and snowsuits," she said. "They live in old buildings and they wear ragged clothes like Little Orphan Annie."

"Finders keepers, losers weepers," said Mary Beth. "First come, first served."

Molly wanted that baby. She wished Mary Beth were right. It would be easy to wheel the baby off to her own home. But what would her mother say? She would be sure to ask her where she got it. And then she'd make her take it back.

Just then a lady stuck her head out of the door and smiled. She picked the baby up and took it inside with her.

"Darn!" said Mary Beth, stamping her foot.

"There are no orphans around here," said Molly.

"You might be right," said Mary Beth. "We'll have to think of something else."

But what? Molly didn't have forever to get this badge. Some of the Pee Wees already had done everything on the list.

"I think," said Mary Beth, "that you will have to rent a baby."

# CHAPTER 4

# The Rented Baby

"**M**y dad rented a car once," said Mary Beth. "And my aunt rents an apartment. You can rent anything. People rent stuff they want for only a little while. Then they return it when they get tired of it."

"Or when they can't afford to buy it," said Molly.

Both things were true for Molly. She

couldn't afford a baby. And she didn't want it forever.

But Molly did not remember seeing any sign that said BABY FOR RENT. Not in the newspaper ads, or the yellow pages.

The important thing was, she needed a temporary baby. And if she couldn't rent one, she would have to borrow one.

"I have to borrow a baby," said Molly. "Just until I get my badge. But I want one of my own. I don't want to share." Molly remembered Jennifer and didn't want a used baby. One that Mary Beth had already fed and dressed better than she could.

The girls sat down on Molly's front steps and thought about where there was a leftover baby. A baby that no one was using to get a badge. While they were thinking, Rachel came by with her curls bouncing.

"I got a perm," she said. "At the beauty parlor."

"It's nice," said Mary Beth. "Molly needs a baby to get her badge."

"I've already got a baby," said Rachel. "One of my very own. No one else can use her for their badge."

"I don't want your old baby," said Molly.

"Rhonda's just like my little sister except I don't have to share a room or anything," Rachel added.

While the girls sat and thought, Roger and Kevin rode up on their bikes. Mary Beth asked if they knew of a spare baby.

Molly wished Mary Beth would stop asking everyone who came down the street to help her.

"Sonny doesn't need two," said Roger. "Why don't you use one of the twins?"

"But they're brand-new," said Rachel doubtfully. "Mrs. Stone doesn't want to give up a new baby."

"It's not like she's *giving* it to her," said Kevin. "All you need is to feed it a couple of times."

"New mothers need all the help they can get," said Mary Beth. "Those twins will probably drive Sonny's family crazy until they get a schedule."

"Let's go ask her!" said Molly, jumping up.

The Scouts all rushed over to Sonny's house. Before his mother even opened the door, they could hear loud sounds of babies crying.

Larry opened the door. Sonny was there with his fingers in his ears. He looked like he was crying too. His mother was heating two bottles of milk on the

stove. Toys were everywhere. Boxes with bows, and little bibs, and car seats and baby swings were in the kitchen. It didn't look like Sonny's house at all.

"Your mama heating your bottle?" whispered Roger to Sonny, giving him a poke.

Sonny gave Roger a hit on the arm.

"Of course you can tend one of the babies!" said Mrs. Stone when Molly asked her.

"Take them both," said Larry, laughing.

Sonny looked mad. He gave the car seat a kick.

Mrs. Stone winked at the Scouts. "He's a little bit *j-e-a-l-o-u-s*," she spelled.

Molly wondered why she was spelling. Sonny wasn't the smartest one in her class, but he was in second grade and he knew how to spell.

**41**

"I am not jealous!" shouted Sonny, running to his room and slamming his door.

"Now the Stones have three babies instead of one!" whispered Roger to Molly.

"Why don't you come back in an hour or so," said Mrs. Stone to Molly. "When things quiet down a little. Then you can help me, and I can help you get your badge."

Molly wanted to hug Mrs. Stone! The Scouts left, and Molly ran home to tell her mother.

"What a good idea!" said Mrs. Duff. "I know Louise can use you. Be very careful to hold your arm under the baby's head."

"I will," said Molly.

Her worries were over. In another hour she'd tend her own borrowed baby. And be able to get her badge with the others.

Molly watched the clock. As soon as the hour was up she started for the Stones'. She pictured herself rocking Lani. And cuddling her. Maybe putting her little sweater and coat on and taking her for a walk in the stroller. Lani would smile at her and coo and reach for her finger, the way she had at the baby shower.

Molly went up to the door. It was quiet. There was no baby crying.

She rang the bell. All of a sudden there was a lot of crying. Crying and screaming. Sonny came to the door.

"Hello, baby kidnapper," he said.

"I'm not a kidnapper," said Molly.

"Go get your own baby," said Sonny, slamming the door in Molly's face.

In a few minutes Larry came to the door.

"Excuse Sonny," he said. "He's having a hard time adjusting."

**43**

"They're my babies!" Sonny shouted. "For my badge."

"You don't need both of them," said Molly.

Molly wondered how Sonny could even tend one of them, he was such a baby himself. A baby will hate him, thought Molly.

Sonny went over to Lani's crib. He reached down and picked her up. Larry stood beside him. Molly wanted to shout, "That's my baby! You take care of Lee." But she didn't. A full-time brother had more power than a part-time mother.

Instead of crying louder, Lani looked up and smiled at Sonny. She even said, "Goo goo." He rocked her back and forth in his arms. She closed her eyes and went back to sleep. Then Sonny put her back in her crib and covered her with a little blanket with roses on it.

Mrs. Stone came in with a pile of clean diapers.

"Can I take care of Lee?" asked Molly.

Sonny walked over to Lee's crib and patted him on the back. He pulled the blanket up over his little shoulders.

"Either one, dear," said Mrs. Stone.

Molly wanted to shout out she needed her own baby. One Sonny didn't take care of. But Mrs. Stone didn't seem to understand that. It looked as if she would have to share with Sonny.

"They didn't finish their bottles," said Mrs. Stone. "When they wake up, we'll let you feed them the rest."

"Fine," said Molly politely. It wouldn't do to fight over which baby. Molly might be asked to leave and then she wouldn't have any baby at all, or any badge.

Larry brought in a can of soda pop for

Molly. When she finished it, Lee began to fuss. Mrs. Stone showed Molly how to heat his bottle. Molly tested it on her arm. What if it was too warm? What if it burned Lee's mouth? Mrs. Stone seemed to trust her! She didn't check it herself. Now Molly was really worried.

"You just sit down and I'll hand you Lee," she said.

Molly began to get nervous. What if she dropped him? What if his head rolled away?

Mrs. Stone put the baby in Molly's arms. He did not look up at Molly and smile. He did not coo. He did not fall asleep. What he did was scream. He screamed as if Molly were sticking a pin into him!

Mrs. Stone had gone into the kitchen.

"Give me that baby," demanded Sonny. "He doesn't like you."

It was true. Lee did not seem to like Molly. Not at all. But Molly was not about to give him to Sonny. She rocked him in her arms. He didn't feel soft and cuddly. He felt stiff and nervous. She sang "Rock-aby Baby" to him. He screamed louder.

Sonny tried to get him out of her arms. Molly held on. Sonny pulled at his legs.

"He's mine!" Sonny shouted. "You're making him cry."

Mrs. Stone came in and said, "You'll have your turn later," to Sonny.

She's too nice to Sonny, thought Molly. She should give him a whack. Tell him to stop being a spoiled brat.

"Here, Molly, this may help," said Mrs. Stone, giving Molly the bottle of warm milk.

Molly put the nipple in Lee's mouth. Lee spit it out. She put it in. He spit it out. Then he got red in the face and yelled.

Finally Mrs. Stone had to take the baby and feed him herself.

"See," whispered Sonny. "He hates you."

"He's just not used to you yet," said Mrs. Stone. "It takes time. Come by tomorrow afternoon and we'll try again. Sonny dear, will you let Molly out?"

Sonny gave Molly a push through the front door. "Don't come back," he snapped.

Molly felt awful. She had found a baby, and she'd failed. It would be a long time before she took one for a walk in the stroller. Or dressed it. She couldn't even get near one!

And she and Sonny used to be friends. Molly always defended him when the others laughed at him. She used to feel sorry for Sonny. Not anymore. Now it was each Scout for himself.

# CHAPTER 5
# Molly Tries Again

"Did you tend the babies?" asked Mrs. Duff when Molly got home. "Did you feed them and dress them?"

"The babies don't like me," said Molly. "They like Sonny."

Mrs. Duff looked surprised.

"Of course they like you," said her mother. "Little babies don't dislike people."

"They hate me," said Molly.

She ran to her room and slammed the door. It was good she knew that babies were allergic to her. Now she would not make the mistake of having her own babies.

Her mother and father would never have grandchildren. Molly felt sad thinking of her parents without grandchildren to love. Her own grandma loved to visit with Molly. And take her places and buy her new clothes.

At suppertime Molly's dad said, "I hear you frighten small children."

He said it to cheer her up, but Molly's throat tightened and suddenly she was crying. Because it was true.

"Honey, you don't really frighten them," her father said quickly. "Babies just cry to strengthen their lungs. It's nothing you did."

Molly looked doubtful.

"They didn't strengthen their lungs when Sonny held them," she said.

"They know Sonny better," said Molly's mother. "By tomorrow they will know you too."

"Really?" said Molly, wiping her eyes.

"I'm sure of it," said her mom.

"I have an idea," said Mr. Duff. "Why don't you take one of your toys to share with the babies?"

What good ideas her dad had. He was right. Babies liked new toys. They would like it if she shared hers with them. And by tomorrow they would know her better. How silly it was to give up after only one day. Maybe she *would* have children after all.

The next day Molly looked through her old toybox for her favorite childhood toy.

A special toy. One that the babies would be sure to love.

Nothing in the box seemed to be special. There was a ball with no air in it. And a doll with her hair missing. The twins were too young for a puzzle. They were too young for a coloring book.

Then Molly saw the perfect thing to share. It was so perfect that it was not even in the toybox. It was on Molly's bed. It was her teddy bear.

She picked it up and hugged it. Her grandma had given it to Molly on her first Christmas.

But what if the babies spit up on Bosco? What if one put Bosco's ear into his or her mouth?

It was worth the risk. Getting these babies to like her meant she had to go all out. And that included Bosco.

At four o'clock Molly tucked Bosco under her arm and started for the Stones'.

Sonny was at the window looking at her.

Molly felt her muscles tighten up. She had been so sure of herself—until she saw Sonny. He was pressing his face up against the window and making an ugly face at her.

When Molly rang the doorbell, no one answered. Maybe it wasn't just Sonny and the twins who didn't like Molly. Maybe none of the Stones wanted her there!

"Answer the door, Sonny!" Molly could hear his mother shout.

But Sonny wasn't going to let her in.

"Sonny?" called Mrs. Stone again.

But Sonny still stood at the window making faces.

Finally Mrs. Stone came to the door.

"Where in the world is Sonny?" she said as she opened it. "He's probably busy with something and didn't hear me," she said.

Sonny heard his mother, thought Molly. If Molly could hear her outside, Sonny could hear her two rooms away.

"The twins are in a good mood today," said Mrs. Stone, leading Molly into the nursery. "Just look at them playing."

The twins were in their playpen. They were playing with a toy that swung over their heads. Lee batted it with his little hand and laughed out loud.

Lani pushed a plastic bird around so it spun. She gurgled and cooed.

"You came just in time to give Lee his bottle," said Mrs. Stone. "Why don't you just sit beside them while I heat the bottle. Get to know them."

Molly drew a chair up to the playpen. Lee stopped batting the toy and laughing. He looked at Molly.

Just then Sonny came into the room. He leaned over the playpen and reached out his finger for Lee to grab. Lee began to laugh again.

"Here we are!" said Mrs. Stone.

She handed Molly the bottle of warm milk. Then she picked Lee up and put him in Molly's arms.

Sonny leaned over Molly's shoulder. Her muscles tightened up again. She felt Lee's muscles tighten up too.

He opened his mouth. But not for the nipple. He opened his mouth to scream.

"There, there," said Mrs. Stone, patting Lee on the back.

"There, there," said Sonny, jiggling Lee's foot.

"I know he's hungry," said Mrs. Stone, looking puzzled.

Molly wanted to yell, Why don't you all go away and let me alone? But she didn't. After all, Lee was only a borrowed baby.

Mrs. Stone picked up the baby and he stopped crying. He drank the whole bottle of milk.

"It takes time," said Lee's mother. "Maybe you could talk to him while I clean up the kitchen. He's happy now that he is fed."

Lee was happy. Until Mrs. Stone left the room.

"Hi, Lee!" said Molly brightly, leaning over the playpen the way Sonny had. "Patty-cake, patty-cake, baker's man," she went on.

Lee began to cry.

Sonny sat on the couch and smiled a wicked smile.

Now was the time to give Lee her teddy bear.

She picked Bosco up off the table and leaned down over the baby.

"Look!" she said, waving the bear's paw at him. "This is Bosco. He wants to play with you."

Lee stopped crying for a second and looked at the bear.

Then he began to cry all over again, only louder.

"Ha, ha, Bosco!" said Sonny. "What a dumb name for a bear!"

Molly held the bear closer to Lee. Lee grabbed the bear and threw it. He threw it over his head.

"How are we doing?" said Mrs. Stone, putting her head through the doorway. "Is he being a good boy?"

"Molly's making him cry with her old bear," said Sonny.

When Molly walked away from the playpen, Lee stopped crying.

When she got close, he began again.

Molly began to feel as if she were wearing poison underwear.

"We can't rush these things," said Mrs. Stone. "Why don't we dress the twins and take a little walk?"

Mrs. Stone dressed them. When Molly tried to help, Lee bit her.

Their mother put them into the double stroller. She tied their caps under their chins. They were ready to go.

When Mrs. Stone pushed the stroller, the twins cooed.

When Sonny pushed it, they gurgled.

And when Molly pushed it, they screamed.

"Here," said Mrs. Stone. "Just slide your hand over and we'll push it together."

The twins didn't cry.

"That's because they can't see you," said Sonny. "If they don't turn around, they don't know it's you that's pushing them."

They went around one block and returned to the house. Molly helped carry the stroller inside. She said she had to leave. No one argued with her.

"Come again tomorrow, dear," said Sonny's mother.

But her voice didn't sound sincere. No mother would want a baby-tender who made her babies cry, thought Molly.

"Good-bye," said Molly, relieved to be going out the door.

When she got to the bottom of the steps, the door opened.

"And take this," said Sonny, throwing her teddy bear through the air toward her.

It landed on the snowy ground.

Molly picked it up. One leg was missing! And she knew the babies had not done it.

# CHAPTER 6

# Back to the Stones'

When Molly got home, her dad was already home from work.

"How did it go today, babe?" he asked.

"Were the twins in a better mood today?" asked her mom.

"They were until they saw me," said Molly.

Molly didn't want any supper.

She didn't want to talk about babies.

She didn't want to think about badges.

She wasn't even sure she wanted to be a Pee Wee Scout!

Now she was sure the babies hated her. More time wouldn't help any.

Molly went to her room and curled up on her bed. After a while her mother tapped on her door.

"Here's some dinner for you, Molly," she said. Molly didn't answer.

She set a tray down on Molly's dresser.

"You can eat here in your room," she added.

"I'm not sick," said Molly.

When she was sick, her mother brought a tray to her room.

After her mother left, Molly ate a little of her meat loaf.

And she ate a little of her apple pie.

The world wasn't going to end just because a baby didn't like her.

*  *  *

The next day was Tuesday. Pee Wee meeting day.

Everyone there had tended a baby.

"I took my little brother for a long walk," said Kenny.

"I protected my baby from a big dog," said Lisa.

"Rhonda's teething and I bought her a teething ring," said Rachel. "She liked it."

Even Roger had fed his little cousin some rice cereal. Roger! How could a baby like Roger?

"You are all doing very well," said Mrs. Peters, smiling.

Sonny's hand was waving.

"Molly isn't," he cried. "My babies don't like Molly."

"I'm sure that is not true," said Mrs. Peters.

"Yes it is!" shouted Sonny. "They hate her!"

"It takes time," said their leader. "You can't learn to tend a baby in one day."

"I did," said Kevin. "I did it all in one day."

"So did I," said Rachel.

"Well, Molly can take her time, there is no rush," said Mrs. Peters. "And now we will talk about all the good deeds we have done the last two weeks."

Molly was glad that Mrs. Peters had changed the subject.

But when the Scouts told about their good deeds, they all seemed to have to do with babies!

"I pushed the cart at the market. When our baby grabbed stuff off the shelves, I put it back," said Tracy.

Mrs. Peters nodded. "Very good," she said.

**67**

Hands were waving.

"Mrs. Peters, I picked up baby toys that were all over the floor," said Tim.

"I taught my baby to say 'bye-bye,' " said Patty. "He can say four words now."

When was this going to end? thought Molly. Didn't anyone ever do good deeds for grown-ups? Babies weren't the only ones in the world.

"Molly?" said Mrs. Peters. "What good deed did you do this week?"

"I matched up all the socks when they came out of the dryer," she said.

Everyone stared at her.

"They were all stuck together," she added. "It took a long time."

"Your mom should use Jump," said Kevin. "My mom does. You put these little sheets in the dryer and then there's no static. Even the diapers don't stick to things."

They were back to babies.

The Pee Wees played games and ate cupcakes.

Mrs. Peters showed them pictures in a baby-tending book.

Then they said their pledge and sang their song.

"One more week to hand in the things you did to tend a baby," Mrs. Peters said. "And then we have to get ready for the holidays."

"Do you want to feed Jennifer?" asked Mary Beth on the way home.

"No!" shouted Molly. Jennifer was sure to hate Molly too. And besides, she had already told Mary Beth she would get her own baby. She didn't want to come crawling back and beg for Jennifer now.

"What are you going to do?" demanded Roger. "You won't get your badge."

"So what?" said Molly, turning in at her own house.

At dinner her mother said, "I don't think you should give up, Molly. You know Rome wasn't built in a day."

What did giving up have to do with Rome?

"No one likes a quitter," said her dad, passing Molly the potatoes.

Molly had never thought of herself as a quitter. She had always worked at something until she got it right. She couldn't give up now.

"Try once more," said her mother. "Give Lani and Lee another chance."

After school on Wednesday, Molly stopped at the Stones'.

She didn't call first.

She didn't bring a teddy bear.

And she didn't feel nervous.

She felt mad.

No baby was going to get the best of her.

When she knocked on the door, Larry answered.

"Come in," he said. "Can you hold Lani while I answer the phone in the kitchen?"

Sonny was not home.

Mrs. Stone was not home.

Molly took Lani.

She did not worry about dropping her. Or at least, not a lot.

She did not worry about Lani's head falling off.

She just held the baby firmly and gave her a big hug.

Molly even walked around the house with Lani. She showed her the snowman from the front window. She told her she was a pretty baby.

And Lani smiled.

# CHAPTER 7

# Molly Saves the Day

By the time Larry came back, Lani was laughing.

"Can I give her a bottle?" asked Molly.

"You bet," said Larry. "I'll go heat it. I can use all the help I can get today. Louise and Sonny have gone Christmas shopping."

Larry heated the milk. Lee began to cry and Molly carefully put Lani down in her crib and picked up Lee. She rocked him back and forth in her arms and walked to the window. She showed him the snowman too. He stopped crying.

"Here we are," said Larry. "You can feed Lee and I'll feed Lani."

Molly sat down and gently put the bottle nipple in Lee's mouth.

He did not spit it out.

He did not start to cry.

He looked up at Molly and smiled, and drank his milk.

When both babies had finished their milk, Molly helped Larry change their diapers. Feeding babies was definitely a better job than diapering them, thought Molly.

Then Molly played with the babies while Larry washed dishes and swept the kitchen. He put a load of diapers into the washing machine. Molly was glad he did not ask her to help with that. By the time he was through, both babies were asleep in their cribs.

"You are a good baby-tender," said Larry. "You should get two badges. One for each baby. And maybe one more for saving the day for a new dad."

"At first the babies didn't like me," said Molly. "They both cried when I held them."

"I think you were nervous," said Larry. "Babies can sense when you are afraid to pick them up. That happened to me when they first arrived. I was afraid I'd drop them and I was afraid their heads would fall off. They screamed when they saw me."

"Really?" said Molly.

Larry nodded.

Why didn't Mrs. Stone tell her that this had happened?

Why hadn't she told her their own father made them cry too?

Molly knew that Sonny made her nervous too. And today Sonny wasn't here.
She wouldn't tell Larry about Sonny. He
might feel bad that he had such a mean
person for a son. But she knew it was
true. Baby-tending was better when
Sonny and Mrs. Stone were gone.

Larry got out some cookies and milk for
Molly.

When she was ready to leave, she gave
the babies each a little kiss.

"Thank you, Molly," said Larry. "You
did a great job helping out."

What wonderful words! She was a help
to Larry! She'd get her badge after all!
And wonder of wonders, the babies did
like her.

Molly skipped through the snow all the
way home.

76

She burst in the back door of her house with red cheeks.

"They like me!" she called to her mother. "The babies like me!"

"Of course they do," said her mother. "I told you so."

Molly ran up to her room. She called Mary Beth and told her the good news.

"That old Sonny," said Mary Beth. "It was all his fault. He's the one who made you nervous. The babies liked you all along."

"He was jealous," said Molly. "After all, they are his babies."

Molly was feeling kinder toward Sonny now that she knew she'd get her badge. Maybe if she had a baby of her own, she wouldn't want to share it either.

But I wouldn't be so mean, she thought.

The next Pee Wee meeting was the last one before the holidays.

Everyone had tended a baby. Everyone had handed their list in to Mrs. Peters.

"Today is the day we make gifts," said their leader. "Isn't it nice that we all have something to give?"

Mrs. Peters looked at Molly when she said that. Mrs. Peters had been worried, thought Molly. Worried that Molly would be the only one who couldn't tend a baby. The only one who wouldn't have that gift to give. But she did.

The table in Mrs. Peters's basement was covered with bright-colored paper. Red and green and white and blue. There were scissors and paste at each place.

The Pee Wees sat down. Mrs. Peters showed them how to cut and fold a big card.

"You can draw a picture of anything you like on it," she said. "It can be a Christmas picture or a Hanukkah picture or a baby-tending picture. Inside we will write these words," she said, writing them on the blackboard. " 'I will help take care of your baby during vacation. Happy holidays! Love, ———.' "

"The whole vacation?" called Roger in alarm. "I have to take care of screaming kids during my vacation?"

"It sounds like Roger's baby didn't like him either," said Rachel to Molly.

What did Rachel mean, "either"? Molly's babies *had* liked her.

"Not all of vacation, Roger. Just as often as you want to," said their leader.

"One minute," said Roger. "I'm going to write 'I'll tend your baby for one minute.' "

Soon everyone was hard at work. There were babies on the cards. And Santas and menorahs. There were holly leaves and holly berries and fat snowmen. There were Christmas trees and candles.

"Look," said Tracy. "Look at Tim's card."

Tim had drawn a racing car on his card.

"That's not a holiday picture," scoffed Rachel.

"It is too," said Tim. "It's a picture of what I want for Christmas."

No one could argue with that.

"Mrs. Peters," called Rachel. "I am going to give this gift to my aunt. But what will I give to my parents?"

Molly had wondered that too. If she gave her card to the Stones, she would still need a gift for her parents.

"That's a good question, Rachel," said

Mrs. Peters. "Those who tended someone else's baby can make two cards. One for the baby's parents, and one for your own parents. Perhaps you can think of some other good deed you can do for your own parents, if there is no baby. Maybe you can help get Christmas dinner, or help wash and dry the dishes afterward."

"We have a dishwasher," said Rachel.

"We're going out for dinner," said Kevin.

"Well, there are many things you can do that your parents would like," she added. "Just think awhile."

Molly decided she would peel apples for their Christmas pie. That could be for her mother and father and even her grandma. They all liked apple pie.

She drew a picture of herself peeling the apples. Inside, she drew a picture of the pie with steam coming out of the top of it.

"Ho," said Roger. "You should peel pumpkins. Pumpkin pie is what you have for the holidays."

"You don't peel pumpkins," said Lisa.

"What do you do, then, eat them with the skin on?" asked Roger.

"You get them out of a can," said Tim.

While Molly was working on her cards, Sonny came up behind her.

He slipped a little red piece of paper in front of her.

It was a little card. On the front it had a picture of a teddy bear with one leg missing. Inside, it said *I'll buy you a new bear. Sonny.*

It didn't say *I'm sorry*, but it meant the same thing, thought Molly.

"That's okay," said Molly to Sonny. "My mom can fix it."

Molly was glad Sonny had given her the card. She didn't like to lose friends. She didn't like to think of Sonny as mean. She hoped he had saved Bosco's leg.

The Scouts made envelopes out of white paper for their cards. It wasn't easy. No one's flaps folded the right way. But Mrs. Peters helped. And Mrs. Stone came over and helped too.

When they had finished, they told about good deeds. Then they had cupcakes with red frosting. And then Mrs. Peters said, "And now we will give out the new badges!"

The Pee Wees shivered with excitement. Molly got goose bumps every time new badges were given out.

Mrs. Stone called out the names and Mrs. Peters pinned on the badges. They were in the shape of a diaper pin. Everyone got one.

When all the Scouts had their badges, everyone clapped. Then they said their pledge and sang their song.

"Happy holidays!" everyone called as they got their coats on.

"Happy baby-tending!" said Mrs. Peters as they went out the door.

And it would be, thought Molly. When a baby smiled, and his head didn't roll off, baby-tending was as happy as happy could be!